MW01168691

IMPOSSIBLE
DRIVEWAYS

JUSTIN GRIMBOL

ATLATL

Atlatl Press
POB 521
Dayton, Ohio 45401
atlatlpress.com

Impossible Driveways
Copyright © 2018 by Justin Grimbol
Cover image copyright © 2018 by Justin Grimbol
Cover design copyright © 2018 by Squidbar Designs
ISBN-13: 978-1-941918-38-8

This book is a work of fiction. Names, characters, business organizations, places, events, and incidents either are the product of the author's imagination or are used fictitiously. The author's use of names of actual persons (living or dead), places, and characters is incidental to the purposes of the plot, and is not intended to change the entirely fictional character of the work.

No part of this work may be reproduced, stored in a retrieval system, or transmitted by any means without the written permission of the author or publisher.

IMPOSSIBLE
DRIVEWAYS

Also By Justin Grimbol

Drinking Until Morning

The Crud Masters

The Party Lords

The Creek

Naked Friends

Hard Bodies

Minivan Poems

Come Home, We Love You Still

Mud Season

MY DOG KEPT barking at things hiding in the woods. I wondered if somebody was out there. I wondered if they were wearing sweatpants. I was wearing sweatpants.

I CUT LOGS of wood with a hatchet. I made the wood smaller. Then I burnt my finger on the wood stove. Then I drank some diet soda.

DAY 3 IN the cabin. It snowed all night. And our heat stopped working.

We woke up cold.

It was still dark.

I messed around with the thermostat. It was one of those devices that looked like it might have looked futuristic in the early nineties. But now it was just a mess of buttons. So many buttons.

"It's broken," I said. "We're screwed."

I had a hissy fit.

Then Bella had one.

Then I had another one. I was an anxious guy. I could have more hysterical hissy fits than most people. And that morning, with all the snow and the broken thermostat, I felt like I was lost in the arctic.

So much anxiety. My hands were sweating. I wasn't blinking much.

The darkness loosened. The early morning light was cold and blue. I started to feel a little better. Not much though.

I waited until eight to call technical support. The kid on the phone seemed a little stoned. I liked that. The situation needed a stoner. It needed the mind of an overworked ganja wizard. His voice sounded gentle. I would have done anything for him right then. I would have done anything he asked.

First, he had me take the control panel off. I described to him the two wires I saw. He taught me how to connect the wires using a safety pin. The heater turned on for a moment. I was thrilled. I felt like MacGyver. The stoned dude told me my furnace was working fine, but the thermostat was fucked. I needed to buy a new one.

At this point I was feeling handy, even though we had not actually gotten anything done.

I was still anxious though. I mean, I couldn't get the heat situation off my mind.

I spent the rest of the morning gathering wood, chopping it up, wishing I had gloves, then getting a fire started in our wood stove. It took a while, but I managed to start a decent fire.

By noon the house was a toasty seventy degrees.

At one in the afternoon, the heater came back on. My wife and I laughed. It got up to eighty-seven degrees.

Bella wanted to turn it down. I told her not to. I felt it would jinx the thermostat in some way. If it went to sleep it would never wake up again.

MY DRIVEWAY WAS steep and slippery. Our cars were parked at the bottom. I needed to get down there but the driveway was intimidating. It was anxiety producing. I was sure I was going to slip and fall on my butt, my tender thirty-five-year-old butt. My wife woke up early to go to work. I imagined her falling and breaking her leg. She would call out to me, but I wouldn't be able to hear her. And she would die. I thought about this a lot. This driveway was a lousy kind of adventure. It reminded me that I was old and balding and hefty and yawn too often. That was the sound of puberty scars fading.

I USED A long rake to scrape the roof of the cabin. My arms hurt. I had never done this before. I suffered from too much never-done-this-before. Also, gloves would have helped.

THE PLOW CAME and covered my driveway in dirt. So, I thought I could drive up the thing. But I was wrong. I only got about halfway up. Then I started sliding backwards.

The car turned. It got angled so I had no way to maneuver the thing without getting even more stuck.

After cursing and screaming for a while, I got out of my car and saw the back hanging over the ledge. My dog and I stared at our situation.

I had a hissy fit. I cursed and kicked the car and just as I was about to start weeping, a truck pulled up. I waved, trying to be both friendly and hopeless looking. This pudgy guy in a camouflaged snowsuit got out.

He asked if I needed help. I did.

8

He asked if I had a chain. I didn't.

I didn't have a chain or a rope or anything like that. I didn't even have gloves. He breathed in and let the air out slowly. Then he attached our vehicles with neon green straps. He worked a lever that tightened the straps.

"Don't just stand there," he said. "Get over there and push. Push like a motherfucker."

I put my back up against the car and pushed. It moved a bit. Then a bit more.

"Push harder!" he yelled. "Wobble it back and forth. I mean really wobble it hard!" he yelled.

I kept pushing and wobbling it and groaning and sounding like I was on coke and finishing hours of bad sex. I felt self-conscious about my grunting and panting, but it was hard to hold it all in. The car budged some more.

The guy walked over and helped me push. I saw the tire lift and drop.

"Did you just pick up my car?" I asked.

"Just a little," he said.

"Living in Vermont is really good exercise, isn't it?"

"Sure is."

OUR CAR STILL couldn't make it up our driveway. It was too steep. Too slippery. Even after it got plowed, even after it got sanded, our jeep made it about halfway up, then started sliding backwards. We had no furniture. I had to buy furniture then get the furniture up this stupid hill. I told my wife we should furnish our cabin with beanbag chairs. She got sad. So I said I was just joking around. No grown ass man would ever actually want to furnish his home that way.

MY WIFE TURNED thirty. So old. Ancient, really.

Before becoming old, she loved cabins and coffee and dancing badly and kissing badly and naked times and snow storms and the cold ocean of Maine and she loved Christmas cards and seeing pictures of her friends' children and getting drunk and making fun of me and how I make fun of her and just ball-busting in general and she was kind of a nag and she was either too responsible or a complete flake and she loved apologies and I mean she really loved when I told her I'm sorry about something and she loved when I gave her a book to read but she mostly loved watching sitcoms with me and laughing hard and she loved that I cried so easily and she loved catching me crying and she loved laughing at me and she especially loved watching *Roseanne* because I told her my mom was a lot like Roseanne and she never got to meet my mom because my mom is a dead mom and my wife loved hearing about how rowdy my mom was because my wife loved all things rowdy but she also loved being cozy and when we visited her family we hung out with her brother and watched *Seinfeld* and she loved this and she loved family and she also loved vacations and dive bars and red wine and she loved watching our dog run in the woods and she loved when our dog found a stick that was way too large and tried to drag it around and she loved cuddling with this dog and all dogs really and she loved looking at other dogs online and showing me pictures and trying to convince me to buy another dog and she loved Vermont and she was very glad we moved here to this cabin surrounded by cold trees. She loved all those things. She loved these things too much. And I had a feeling she would keep loving these things or at least most of those things.

I ORDERED AN inflatable chair. It should be easy to carry up the driveway. I also bought a dog bed. But my dog doesn't like it much. Right now, she is sitting on my desk chair and I'm sitting on the dog bed trying to feel poetic.

I WOKE UP to scratching sounds coming from the kitchen. I investigated and found some mouse turds. After smoking a cigarette, I went back to bed. I heard the mice again. This time they were overhead in the attic space.

I stood up and punched the ceiling.

I waited. Luckily, due to my trigger-happy anxiety, I was determined. I could wait. I could blend with silence and the shadows.

The mice started running around again.

"MOTHERFUCKERS!" I yelled.

I punched the ceiling and woke my wife up.

"What the hell are you doing?"

"Don't get mad at me! We have mice!"

"We have what?"

"Mice."

"Jesus. Relax, would you. I'm trying to go to sleep."

"You relax."

"You woke me up. I'm grumpy about that. I have to go to work in the morning. Just stop punching the ceiling."

"Fine."

I got into bed.

I couldn't hear the mice. I think Bella scared them off.

I CAME HOME late and parked at the bottom of my impossibly icy driveway. I walked up to the cabin in the complete darkness. I didn't have a flashlight. And there were no stars and no moon. Also, I don't think there is other life in the universe. It's just us. Then, out there, a lot of planets and stars and maybe a worm or two and that's probably it.

MY WIFE, BELLA, and I wanted to get out and bond with our community, so we drove to Bellows Falls and went to the Opera House, which also doubles as a movie theater. *Star Wars* was playing, and the place was packed. One of my wife's coworkers was working the ticket booth so we got in for free.

The movie was supposed to start at six.

At seven the manager came out and walked in front of the screen and told us the projector was not working.

A small deeply teenaged boy yelled, "Fuck you!"

Everyone laughed. Even the manager laughed.

Then there was some booing and more
laughter.

My wife and I got up and left.

It was cold and dark and Bellows Falls
looked empty. Everyone was in the
theater heckling the manager.

"I actually had a really nice time,"
Bella said.

"Same here," I said.

We got in our car and headed home.

That night I thought I had caught one
of the mice. I checked the trap.

It was empty.

WE TOOK THE trash down the hill on a sled. I tried to convince my wife to just let the trash go. Let it slide down the hill. Let it have a good time. She called me a dummy. Then we bickered about something. We put the trash near the mailbox. Then we walked back up the hill.

THE PEOPLE AT the co-op in Putney were fancy. There was a kid playing ukulele while he stocked shelves. It was okay. My wife and I could still argue in the middle of this. We could still say harsh things. We could treat the place like a shed we were locked in.

I PUT BRIE in the mouse trap. My fancy cheese lured a mouse into the trap. Now I had to get rid of the sweet little beast. I'd heard if you don't take the trapped mouse at least two miles away from your cabin, it will find its way back. But it was snowing. So I just walked it down to the bottom of the driveway and dumped it into the snow. It was dead. Poor thing had eaten too much fancy cheese.

THERE WAS A store in Brattleboro
that had a bunch of decent used
furniture. We found a few couches we
liked. The first one was blue. It might
have been the bluest couch I had ever
seen. But it looked stainless and
durable and it was very cheap. Then I
sat on the thing. It was a bad couch.
The fabric felt like it had been washed
too many times. And the cushions felt
less like couch cushions and more like
stuffed animals won at a carnival. We
shopped around some more. The next
couch had this nice brown plaid
design. Bella hated it.

"I veto that couch," she said.

We shopped around some more. Most
of the couches were either too dusty or
had stains that, though usually small,
made us feel a deep sadness.

Finally, we found one we both liked. It looked like something an extremely old lady had taken good care of for a long, long time. And after a brutal fight that made me reconsider every life choice I have ever made, my wife and I decided to buy the couch. We paid the guy. He gave our money a long uneasy look. He acted like our money was a ball of pubic hair. I thought the transaction felt sketchy. My wife assured me he wasn't being sketchy at all. He was just stoned. That made sense to me. The place did smell nice regardless of all the stains.

I BOUGHT AN ugly painting from a thrift store. Then I put it in a stack of other ugly paintings I own.

Bella and I almost fought about money. But then we managed not to.

I also managed not to eat pizza, which was good because I was on a diet.

It was an unseasonably warm day. Snow melted. The creek by our cabin had grown and become loud. The mist was so thick. Last time I drove through something like this Bella and I were young and moving across the country. We were looking for a motel. Our GPS took us on a terror ride through steep mountains. It was supposed to lead us to a cheap motel. Instead it brought us to an empty field in the middle of nowhere.

RICH LADIES LIVE in Vermont too. One told me to pull my pants up and this upset me and I wanted to moon them. I wanted to moon the world and affect the tides. Instead I just pulled my pants up a little and walked my dog.

FOR A WHILE, we couldn't find our trash bin. We grieved. We were sad about having to get a new one. It seemed like an awful thing to have to do. But then, one morning, my wife saw it in the creek across the street. It had blown all the way across the street and down an icy hill into the black stream that flowed there. Bella and I climbed down and retrieved the bin and placed it into the imprint it had left in the snow next to our mailbox. We felt good about this. We felt like we needed to celebrate. So, we got some Thai food in Brattleboro. I was surprised by how much I liked that little city considering how tacky and hip it could be.

After Thai food we went to a coffee shop. It was filled with young people with tattered clothing and colorful hair. They all seemed uptight and awful to me.

"When did punks become so soft spoken and polite?" I said as we walked around the city. "I hate it."

I started making gagging sounds.

"Stop!" Bella said. "You are having way too many responses to things."

MY INFLATABLE CHAIR broke. I mean, it deflated.

"At least it was cheap," I said.

"Who are you kidding," Bella said. "That thing cost a fortune."

"No way, it was only twenty bucks."

"But you had to buy a pump for it."

"So that's still only forty bucks."

"But it also was really ugly and made out of air."

"Air is really fragile."

I wanted to celebrate the demise of my inflatable chair, but Bella didn't like that idea so we just went to bed and in the morning I woke up ready to face the day and to eat a spoonful of peanut butter for breakfast.

TO PROMOTE MY new book, *Idiot's Guide to Dry Humping*, I attended a writing conference in DC. I sold some books and met some folks and managed not to act too desperate. I wanted to grab people by the sleeve as they walked by and yell at them: "Buy my books! They're good books! Please! Just give them a chance! I worked so hard! Why don't you like my books? Is it my beard? Is it my man boobs? Please just be nice to me! Be fair! I love you!" But I held myself together. I just smiled, and when people stopped by, I asked them about their interests.

I made a little money. Not much. But some.

I liked DC. It's a classy looking place. After the writing convention, I wanted to stick around. Keep mingling. See some monuments. But I left early because I had to beat a snow storm coming to Vermont.

I drove straight through and managed to get home at two in the morning. My dog was excited. She stomped her feet and wagged her tail and grunted and whimpered and brought me a sock. A dirty sock. She had found a dirty sock and she wanted to show me because she is my dog and she loves me.

But I am getting ahead of myself. I need to tell you that on my way down to the conference I checked into a seedy motel in NJ. I felt resourceful because the motel was only thirty bucks. As I was smoking a cigarette I was approached by two women who looked like mean boxing coaches, like Mickey in the Rocky movies. We chatted. They offered me sex for money. Called it "a nice night in their apartments."

I was polite.

"No," I said. "I'm all set. Thanks though."

They walked away. Then they came back five minutes later.

"I think we had a misunderstanding before," one of them said to me. "My friend here will fuck you for twenty bucks."

"That's nice. But really, I'm all set. Have a good night."

Later I heard them prowling outside my motel room. I decided to leave and get my money back and find a new motel.

I HAD TO renew my driver's license. Not only did I have to renew it, but I had to switch states. My license was from Wisconsin and I had not lived there in a while. I hated the DMV. They were going to test my vision and see proof of address. I was very worried. What if they got mad at me? What if I lost my license and I couldn't drive any more? Then I would be stuck in the middle of Westminster West in this cabin, ten miles from the closest town.

VERMONT HAD GREAT old people.
We met these two ladies on a hike.
Both had gray hair that was messy
from wind and sweat. They asked us
where we were from. We told them we
had just moved to Westminster West,
near the school house.

"We call that part of town
Westminster West WEST," one of
them said. We had a good laugh. They
seemed a little stoned. I couldn't be
sure. Maybe they were just enjoying
the warm weather.

MY ANXIETY WAS intensifying. I mean I wanted to wear sweatpants all day long, even outside while I stumbled up a mountain, groaning and gasping for breath, or maybe as I'd eat sandwiches at Allen Bros., or as I roamed around an antique store where things smelled like my grandfather who would smoke pipes and let me sit on his lap. When I was a teenager, grandpa had to be moved into a nursing home. My grandmother and I would visit him. He'd take my hand and call me Billy, which is my father's name.

I WENT TO the DMV to renew my license. But they didn't accept my sore throat as a form of identification. I told the dude I would watch a sappy movie and cry in front of him. Would that prove who I am? I mean who I really, really am? But DMV dude said that wouldn't count either.

"What about all this other stuff?" I said. I reached into my pockets and started pulling stuff out. So much stuff flew out of my pockets into the air. So much stuff. Like cigarette butts and scratch off tickets and poetry books and toenail clippings and my social security card and my lease to my cabin and many crumpled dollar bills. All this stuff flew into the air then fell down onto the counter in front of me.

DMV dude told me I needed my birth certificate.

"I forgot that at home," I told him. "It's in a folder. A really organized folder."

He looked at me as if he could see my soul and it was peeing into my ear.

So I went home and instead of finding my birth certificate, I sat on a rocking chair in my front yard. The snow had melted and everything was muddy but still looked kind of nice.

I GOT A job working as a home health aid. To celebrate my first day of work, I battled anxiety like it was a swarm of mosquitoes and dipped a donut in coffee then made grownup grilled cheese sandwiches for my wife.

Long ago, I thought of becoming a minister. Before that, I wanted to be a cartoonist. Before that I wanted to be a slacker teenager (that dream was fulfilled many times over). And when I was a little kid, I wanted to be a bank robber.

MY NEW JOB was not horrible. I visited old people in their homes and helped with daily tasks, like cooking and cleaning and bathing. This was awkward, because as soon as the clients and their family saw me and how sloppy I looked, they knew I was not any good at any of these life skills. I looked like a stray dog, not a professional.

The agency sent me to a guy living in Burtonsville, VT. This man had a real knack for cursing. He told me he was originally from Long Island, which meant he was not a Vermonter. I am also from Long Island. I had migrated to Vermont for college and gotten attached to all the syrupy hippie women, the muddy roads, and the diners.

"You ever miss Long Island?" I asked.

"Fuck no."

"Too crowded, right?"

"I don't like that kind of bullshit."

"You like Vermont?"

He waved his middle finger around
and mumbled something that involved
a lot of curse words.

"Why did you move here?"

"A fucking woman," he said.

Then he laughed.

"So what do you need help with
today?" I asked.

"I don't fucking know."

"You got any laundry?"

"Fuck laundry," he said. "I don't care
about that shit."

I asked him if he wanted me to make
him something for lunch.

"Fuck no," he said.

He pulled out a large hunting knife and cut open a box of cookies and ate a few.

I sat down and relaxed. His apartment was barren. There was nothing on the walls. Just a large window.

"You got a nice view here," I said. "Look at all those fucking trees out there and that creek. It's beautiful."

"It is," he said. "It's very good."

He offered me a cookie. I told him I was on a diet.

After some light cleaning, I headed home. It was snowing so I had to drive slowly.

I kept thinking about his cookies and how badly I wanted to dip those cookies in coffee and eat them. I wanted to eat them until I grew stretch marks.

My grandma used to have cookies like that. She kept them in a round tin. My grandmother loved cookies and hated cursing. She especially hated curse words that referred to sex. She also

41

hated cold weather. And she hated money. "The rich keep getting richer," she would say. "And the poor keep getting poorer." I'm glad she did not live to see a Trump presidency, the most perfect storm of money, greed, and foul language I've ever seen.

Toward the end of her life, my grandmother had become bitter and worn down from being blind, living in federal housing, and having her husband die so slowly and so sloppily.

"You can't tell me this life is blessed," she'd say. She would bitch about things and drink Miller High Life with me. She wasn't a drinker. But during my visits, she would allow herself a few beers. Sometimes she'd even curse and laugh. When I was little, she was a lot of fun. She'd give me gum drops and Twizzlers and soda. Sometimes she'd get really goofy and start singing to me in Danish. And I would dance naked and giggling like I was being tickled by hundreds of guppy-sized ghosts.

As I drove through the messy Vermont roads, I thought about my grandmother and I missed her and I wondered why I cursed in front of her

so much. I felt bad about being so
bratty and rude.

Eventually I got home. My driveway
was too steep and slippery, so I parked
at the bottom and had to walk up to
my cabin. I was surprised to see that
my wife and dog were outside. She
was sitting in a rocking chair we had
left out all winter.

"Hey baby," she said. "Can you believe
this weather? When is spring going to
get here?"

"I know," I said. "It's lousy."

"No, it's not actually that bad. I mean
it's snowing like a motherfucker. But
it's not that bad."

WITH MISMATCHED GLOVES, I
walked down my driveway to dig out
my car. A huge mound of snow stood
in front of it. The snow was heavy and
dense. I shoveled for forty minutes or
so, then noticed a note on the car.

It said, "I went out of my way once to
help. This time I went out of my way
to fuck you." My car had been buried
purposely.

At first, I thought our plow guy was
angry at us. Maybe we had been doing
something rude without realizing it.
Or maybe we owed him money. Most
likely we did. We usually owed
someone money. So I hiked back up to
our cabin and called him. Our plow
guy said he was not mad at us. That
he had no idea about any note. He
called his guys and they didn't know
about the note either.

This made the situation more unsettling. Who had done this? I sat at my computer and thought it over.

A while ago I had gotten my car stuck and this guy pulled over and helped me out. It took a while. And I had wanted to thank him with some money and a six-pack and maybe a copy of one of my books. But I had forgotten his name and the address he gave me. Since we had moved into the cabin, he was the only person who has helped us out in any way. And he had been driving a plow and worked in the area. Had he been expecting money for his trouble? Had he done this?

When I told Bella about the note she freaked out. I didn't know how to calm her down. I also get paranoid and usually without the assistance of an angry note.

We spent a week feeling paranoid. Locking our doors. Telling our neighbors, hoping they might console us in some way. Tell us this happens all the time. Don't worry. It won't happen again. Or maybe it's a sign of affection. But usually they just winced and said, "Oh, shit. That's fucked up, man."

I thought about buying a gun. But they were too expensive. Then I looked into crossbows. Still too expensive. Eventually, I ordered a taser on Amazon.

I immediately regretted spending twenty bucks on a taser. We were broke and twenty dollars could pay for a decent amount of gas or diet soda or egg sandwiches from Saxton River Village Store. And how was I going to know if the thing worked? Was I supposed to test it on myself? I didn't want to do that. I once worked with this girl who had a taser. She tried to show it to me. But the thing had run out of battery.

"Jesus," I said. "How often do you use that thing?"

"I don't know. Sometimes I use it on my boyfriend."

"In a sexual way?"

"No. I use it when he pisses me off. Sometimes he starts these stupid fights with me. He gets me all riled up. Then he tries to walk away. And

I'm like, 'Fuck you. Don't you walk away in the middle of this stupid ass fight.' Then I zap him."

I laughed and felt incredibly impressed and maybe even a little aroused by this slovenly and gutted young woman I worked with.

And now here I was buying my little family a taser. And I think of all the nasty fights my wife and I have had. And I think we would have been better off just tasering each other. Fighting with people you love leaves rust. The kind you find on cars that get abandoned in the woods. The kind that turns into homes for critters and lost dogs.

Over the next week or so I did some detective work. Asked around to see who did it. Got some leads. After a couple days I stopped feeling so anxious about it. I was still locking my doors. But I wasn't really worried.

One day someone told me they knew who helped me out that time. They gave me his name. I looked him up on Facebook. I saw a picture of him with sunglasses and a leather vest, leaning on his motorcycle. I showed my wife.

"That's the guy," I said. "Or at least I think that's the guy."

"Cool," she said. "You going to write to him, ask what happened?"

"Nah."

"That's fine," she said. "You want to have sex before I go to work?"

"Sure."

In the middle of sex she got a cramp. I changed position so we could keep going. We didn't last long, but it was decent sex.

Afterwards she apologized about the cramp.

"I feel bad, like I'm an old lady," she said.

"It really is no big deal," I said. "It didn't bother me at all. It was still nice. You smelled funky and I like that."

"Wait, now you're telling me I smell bad?"

48

"No. You smell funky."

"What the fuck is funky?"

"It means you smell fun."

"Fuck off."

"I mean it."

"You really don't mind that I cramped up?"

"I really don't mind. I'm no gymnast myself."

"That's true."

"Don't be so hard on yourself."

"You are probably right. Still, I would like to be more flexible. Maybe we should both start going to yoga."

"Wait, what the hell are you saying?"

"Yoga. You and I could go to yoga."

"No. I prefer to cramp up."

"You're ridiculous."

"Hey baby . . ."

"What?"

"Do you think that guy's ever going to come back and fuck with us?" I asked my wife.

"No. I doubt it."

I BOUGHT A chair from an antique store. I thought it was perfect but once I got it home I saw how dirty it was. So my wife and I worked it over with a vacuum. We did a few rounds. It was still dirty. After a gentle pat, a dust cloud would erupt from it. We'd cough. And there was hair on the thing. My wife assumed the hairs came from an old lady. I said it probably came from a dog. We bickered about this for a bit, then decided to leave it out on the porch. The next night it rained. It rained hard and for a long time. The rain did not clean the chair. It got really wet. We left it out there to dry. A couple days passed, then it rained again. We have talked about throwing it away. Or leaving it in the shed. But at this point I have gotten kind of used to the thing being there.

I BOUGHT ANOTHER chair from the same antique store. This one looked less dusty. But it still needed some work. So I put it on the porch and vacuumed it for a while. Bella came home and saw the chair. She told me she liked it. She was impressed. It didn't have too many stains. I wanted to flirt with her. Or argue. I couldn't tell. I started sneezing instead. And I kept sneezing all night long. I was allergic to the chair. I was sure of it. And I kept sneezing until I took more than the recommended dose of Claritin. It was a starry night. Also, our dog ran into the dark woods because she saw something and got angry about it. We yelled for her to come back. We didn't want her to leave and not come back or get eaten by a pack of coyotes or something like that. So we yelled. We yelled her name until she came back to us.

WE HAD SOME warm weather. Eerily warm. I did not trust it. I wouldn't let myself get too comfortable with sixty-degree February days. It was going to get cold again. I was sure of it.

Bella loved this warm weather. She loved every minute of it. She was curvy and had dirty blond hair and when I met her she loved to get stoned and pet bumble bees. This woman needed to go out and frolic. To frolic hard. She was an expert frolicker. She frolicked up mountains. She frolicked into cold oceans. She frolicked into trendy bars and down dusty backroads. Sometimes I frolicked with her. I was decent at frolicking. But sometimes I preferred to shop at antique stores for hours at a time.

On one of these warm days, we decided to frolic all the way to our old college in Poultney, Vermont. We loved that town. It was quiet in a way that's hard to find on the east coast.

The town was only an hour or so away. We arrived while it was still morning and we shopped at the used bookstore, got a soda at Stewarts, visited the campus, then walked a small footbridge that crossed the Poultney River. I told her a story about how my buddy Enzo and I once bought a bunch of wine and sat at this bridge and drank and read pretentious Beat poetry out loud all day long. We loved Kerouac's *Mexico City Blues* and Enzo wanted to read the whole book out loud. It took a long time because we got very drunk. At one point, while we were reading, a bunch of other students showed up. They were trying to have a class outside. The bridge was a perfect place for this. Drunk and feeling inspired by corny poems, Enzo and I took over the class and rambled on about poetry and the Beats. For some reason the professor let this happen. We even read some of *Mexico City Blues* to the kids. I imitated Kerouac's voice as I read which must have made me sound doofy and I noticed that all the students looked bored, but I kept reading anyway, acting even more wild, doing my crappy imitation of Kerouac.

Bella laughed hard even though she had heard the story many times.

For lunch, my wife and I got a sandwich at a diner called Perry's. I used to go to this diner frequently when I was a student. My whole being would be sloppy and bruised from drinking boxed wine and snuggling with naked friends. I'd eat an egg sandwich and nurse this hangover and I'd feel happy.

There were no students there that day though. Just old people and I preferred it that way.

We sat at the counter.

"Should we move here one day?" Bella asked.

"You want to move into this diner?"

"No, dumb face, I mean Poultney."

"Sure, I could finish college. We could move into one of the dorms."

"Oh never mind."

The daughter of one of the waitresses came in and sat at the counter between me and a chubby old man in suspenders. She looked young, maybe eight or nine years old. The old man joked with the child. He chatted with her about school and how boring it was. Then the old man helped her build a tower out of creamer cups. The tower became tall and it looked like it could tip over any minute, but they kept working on the thing and it was very fun to watch. I ate my grilled cheese on rye, occasionally dipping it in a cup of soup. Finally, the tower fell and everyone at the counter had a good laugh.

After lunch we walked around some more. Though we loved it there, it was hard to stick around for too long. We made one more lap around town and argued about what we were going to eat for dinner. Both of us agreed we should diet. But I thought we could fit pizza into this diet somehow. She did not agree.

IT WAS SPRING and I wanted to enjoy reading Kerouac again—to sit in the allergy ridden warmth and hear birds and read him and feel excited about it, like when I was in college and naked-cuddling with friends—But it just doesn't work—It's not the same—I've tried, but the books annoy me. Something about them seems needy and wordy and I give up a page or two in and get really sad about it. I don't want to dismiss the dude—he wanted things to be lost but new and I wanted the same things. Transcendence is letting yourself be homesick for a place that does not exist. Pretentious mountains and stuff. Love your friends and get naked with them sometimes.

I WALK INTO the woods behind the
cabin and there are no trails and I get
nervous about being doomed and all
the usual stuff and eventually I find
an old stone wall and I follow it and I
find a waterfall, a small one, and I
find a tree that has fallen over and
turned into a bench and I sit on it and
I watch my dog sniff things and I am
still anxious. I've been so anxious
lately. It gets unbearable. I wonder if
this uneasiness makes everything look
even more beautiful and vivid and I
can't help but to do a crappy job trying
to meditate and then break it down
into a prayer about how I don't want
this all taken away from me. None of
it. Especially my dog. I am way too
attached to my dog. And I follow the
stone wall more and it reminds me of
the stone wall in Burtonsville, NY,
leading to my family's cottage and
then the creek where my grandfather

died with his son in his arms (heart-attack and fatness and death-grip) and where I eventually put my mom's ashes (she died of fatness too) and where I also learned how to swim over and over again. I will have to head there again soon and learn how to swim again, swim full of anxiety and slipping on rocks and being sucked into rapids and laughing some.

MY WIFE AND I hiked up this mountain and tried to meditate, but we ended up fighting instead. We fought about fighting and why we fight and how we fight and all that. So in a way, I guess this was a kind of meditating. And I dog eared books. And I ate boogers. And my dad visited for a week or so and he took us out to a fancy meal in Newfane and we all bickered the whole time and it got emotional. I drank beers. Cheap beers. It felt good to drink cheap beers in a fancy restaurant.

MY ANXIETY WAS getting worse. I felt doomed. I imagined horrible scenarios. Often these fantasies involved my job as a home health aid. I once imagined one of the old guys pulling a gun on me. "Please! I have a wife and children!" I'd beg. "You got no children!" he'd tell me. Then he'd shoot me a bunch. I thought this might actually happen. I was terrified to go to work. But I forced myself to go anyway.

Once a client, an elderly man, asked me to buy him beer. I told him I was not allowed to buy him booze and he got mad. He told me he didn't like me anymore. He told me I was too straight. He called me a nerd. But he didn't shoot me. After that I got worried that I was supposed to buy him beer. If I didn't he could get the DTs and die. I called the nurse who was working the office that day. I asked if I was supposed to buy him beer. The woman laughed. "I doubt buying beer is on his care plan," she said. "You did the right thing."

I had anxiety before. Once it got so bad I had to quit my job and I ended up shaving my head and face and looking like a Hellraiser turtle. I had not seen my jowls in a long time and I was humiliated, and I wept on the floor in front of my wife and punched myself in the face.

I didn't plan on shaving my beard ever again. And I wasn't going to quit this job. I needed something else. Meditation. I had been doing some of that. It helped a bit.

I TRIED TO throw away a soda can I had filled with cigarette butts. Easier said than done. I worried the can of damp cigarettes would somehow self-ignite, or maybe spill onto the floor and poison my dog. I told myself I was being crazy. I even screamed and punched the kitchen table a bit. Then I dug the can out of the trash. I brought it to work with me. I meant to throw it in the trash there, but it spilled as I was driving, making my jeep smell rotten and greasy and sour. Shit, my wife is going to kill me, I thought. I punched myself in the face. Then took the floor mat out. Peed on it. Then let it get soaked in the rain. I took some Febreze from my job and sprayed it in there. It didn't work. I wrote a text to my wife, telling her I was sorry. I didn't tell her why I was sorry. It didn't matter. "Thanks. I love you anyway," she wrote. I wondered what she thought I was apologizing about. Then I let it go.

THOSE GODDAMN DANDELIONS
were everywhere. Early spring.
Minimal lawnmower action. I had
anxiety about this and other stuff. I
felt doomed again and again and
again.

FOR BREAKFAST, I drove around and imagined my dog abandoning me. Maybe I left the door open or something. I only checked the locks five or six times. My dog could have gotten out, then been lured into the woods by a coyote. Then eaten. Or maybe kidnapped by a hillbilly. It was best not to think about doomed things like my dog lonely and whimpering in the woods. I asked this old guy about dogs from the past. He told me about his old lab who ran off a few times. Once, it was gone for a week and eventually found its way home. I felt relieved. My dog will find her way home, I told myself. Even though she hadn't actually left yet. I was pretty sure I closed all the doors and locked them.

I COULD HEAR the coyotes and the wind. I wanted to stay up and read and listen to coyotes and wind and stuff, but the lamp near the bed got too hot and I was afraid it would light everything on fire. So I took the lightbulb out, let it cool down, and threw it away. At one point I woke up in the middle of the night and fondled my wife. She fondled me back. Morning came. Our lawn was overgrown, and the lawnmower was broken. The flowers on the bush outside our cabin had bloomed and it was very pink and reminded me of tights my wife used to wear when we first met.

I FOUND A new dirt road to walk
down with my wife and our dog. It was
the best dirt road we had found so far.
I wanted to walk on this road as much
as I could. I wanted to imitate it. I
wanted to walk on it so often that I
couldn't help but imitate it. A week or
so before, I had gone to my buddy's
wedding. We knew each other as
children and now he was married. He
lived in New York and looked fancy.
At the wedding I got sweaty from
dancing badly and for a long time. His
wife found me. "You and my husband
have the same facial expression and
you kind of talk the same way," she
said. "You know why? It's cause you
grew up together. That happens when
people grow up together." I just
nodded and smiled and took a sip of
my cocktail. That was the kind of
relationship I wanted with that dirt
road. The road that ran along all those
large fields and tall grass.

MY THERAPIST SUGGESTED I start taking some sort of medication to help me deal with my anxiety. For years I had resisted this idea, but at this point the anxiety had become so constant and brutal and scary, I decided to give it a try.

So I went to Otter Creek Associates in Brattleboro to get evaluated. The psychiatrist was tall and freckled and wore a summery dress. As soon as I sat down in her office, I started ranting and explaining my anxiety and all the strange fears. I told her I felt doomed. I told her stories too. I told her about my car accidents and my mom's death. I started flirting. Soon we were both giggling. She looked nice. I wanted her to hold me. I wanted us to sniff each other. Is this transference? I thought. Can it happen that quickly?

She told me about the meds and mentioned they had side effects. Like lowered sex drive.

"Lowered sex drive? Oh, thank God! That sounds great! Please lower my sex drive! Lower my sex drive as much as possible!"

She laughed.

We talked some more. We had some more laughs.

Then she gave me my scripts.

I took them to the Rite Aid, where a few grumpy looking folks worked the pharmacy. I started flirting with them too. Laughter happened. I'm a big sloppy guy, in no way a Casanova, but I loved flirting. Flirting made me feel good about life. Flirting was the opposite of checking to see if the doors were locked. And I had not flirted like this in a long time.

They got me my meds and I took some Ativan immediately.

Then I got an ice cream at Fast Eddie's across the street.

"I'm old fashioned," I told the girl who worked there. "Just give me some vanilla soft serve. Rainbow sprinkles."

"Want a cone?"

"Of course I want a cone. I don't want to just hold the cold ice cream in my hands."

She didn't find that funny. I had run out of charm. This didn't upset me though. I felt okay about being charmless. I was going to eat ice cream. I had some meds that might help me with the brutal anxiety I had been dealing with. I enjoyed the smell of my own stinking armpits and there were storm clouds gathering and looking powerful.

I ate the cone and watched the sky. The temperature dropped some.

I drove a long way home. I traveled around some dirt road, keeping the window open so I could smell the pine trees. It started to rain. Nothing hard. It just drizzled. Those massive clouds looked burly, but this was all they produced.

When I got home I sprawled out on my couch and watched *Star Trek* fan films. *Star Trek* fans had made so many of these things and they were all really bad. One showed a Vulcan, an Orion, and a human dude in bed in what looked like an Econo Lodge. It was supposed to be a space station or maybe a space motel or something, but it just looked like a normal Econo Lodge.

MY WIFE ALREADY looked more like summer than most of the rivers and moths and anxiety meds and lightning bugs and yard sales, and the meds were making me feel a bit edgy, which was not the desired effect, so we went to have a swim for Christ's sake, and it was too cold. Also, we were naked.

I SAW SOME party animals tubing
down the river. They had beer and cigs
and they looked like gym teachers. I
waved to them. I wanted them to
remember me somehow, even though
we had never met before.

One of the tubes carried a stereo
system. A Michael Jackson song came
on. Something from *Off The Wall*.
"YES! THIS IS MY FUCKING JAM!"
one yelled.

There was lots of cheering and singing
and fist pumping.

"Have a fun trip, guys!" I yelled.

They didn't hear me. The party
animals had already floated away
from me. The current was strong.

I WENT FOR a long drive, hoping to calm my mind down some. After a few hours I ended up in Troy, New York. I stopped at a gas station and bought a diet soda and a pack of cigarettes. I smoked. Tossed it out the window. Half an hour later, I started worrying about forest fires. So I turned back around to make sure my cigarette hadn't started anything. I drove for a while because I couldn't remember where I had tossed it. Eventually, I took a couple Ativan and headed home again.

I was tired of being in the car, so I stopped at a park and let my dog walk around a bit. There was a lake and I saw a man in a canoe with his family. He seemed frustrated.

"No!" he yelled. "For the hundredth time. There are no sharks in the lake!"

"But how can you be sure?" one of the kids yelled back.

I WAS TAKING care of this old rich
guy in Esperance, VT, who spent most
of his days nodding off and listening to
soft jazz. I felt peaceful there. Then I
noticed how bad my armpits stank. I
mean, they really stank. Way worse
than usual. I probed them with my
hand, then brought the hand up to my
nose. The smell made my eyes water. I
thought it was kind of sexy. But
absolutely not appropriate for work.

Then the guy's daughter came home.
She walked up to me and shook my
hand. The stinky hand. Well, at this
point I had probed twice so both hands
were stinky. She told me she was
going out to do some errands. I felt
lousy about this. She was going to
wander around smelling like my
armpits.

At one point the old man and I sat out

on the porch. It started to rain. He was asleep. I thought about walking into the rain and washing my armpits some. But as soon as I stood up, the old man's eyes opened and he looked at me like I was an intruder. I smiled and told him he had a beautiful property. He smiled back.

Eventually, my shift ended. I got in my jeep and lit a cigarette and headed home. He had a long driveway that was lined with tall maples. I turned onto Route 35 and I could smell river. My wife was home. We were going to bicker about something. I could feel it in my bones. That meant I would have no time to wash my armpits. Oh well. Maybe I could get to that some other day.

THERE WERE LOTS of moths in our cabin. I didn't mind them most of the time. They were attracted to the light coming from our windows and they snuck inside our cabin and they would try to find light in there. They didn't realize they would also see my wife and I bickering and doing naked things. Sometimes they joined in and flew into my face too often and I had to kill them.

Also, I talked to my aunt for the first time in years. She was in a nursing home. She was sad and wanted us all to live together. My wife, my dad, and me. She wanted us all to live in a place and help each other. I tried to find gentle ways of saying that will never happen. But that I might be able to visit for Christmas.

I SWAM AROUND my favorite swim spot for a while. It was cold. A naked old guy joined me. We talked about farming. I know almost nothing about farming. But I acted interested to be polite and I also tried to not stare at his penis too much for the same reason.

Then I played fetch with my dog for a while. Then I meditated. Then I napped, using my towel as a pillow.

THE NEXT DAY I went back to my favorite swimming hole hoping to find more naked farmers. I sat there a while and waited. I played fetch for a while. With my dog, not with myself. I got a little too into the game and I slipped on the slick rock floor of the creek and hit my head on the roots of an old tree. Blood dripped down my face into the water. I stumbled out of the creek and down the path that led to my car. My dog followed. She acted concerned. When we got in the car, she tried to lick the wound. I pushed her away and looked in the rearview mirror. I had a gash and lump. I cursed a lot and felt scared. I decided to get it checked out.

Urgent Care was still open, so I went there instead of the emergency room. I liked that place. The people who work there acted like they smoked a lot of weed. There was this nurse who had red hair and a nice smile. That day, with my lumpy bleeding head, I flirted with her for a while and told jokes about how I think the wound added to my sex appeal. She laughed and that made me feel good about myself.

Then the doctor came in. He didn't think I needed stitches. Instead he put a bunch of glue on my wound. No bandage. I wanted to hug him and thank him for fixing me. I wanted to strip down and tell him he deserved to see the real me. "I have stretch marks," I'd tell him. "Can you fix them?" Then he would put his hand on my shoulder and we would cry together.

After my visit to Urgent Care, I drove to Rite Aid to buy Tylenol and a bottle of Coke Zero Cherry. Rite Aid always confused me. It was too complicated. I couldn't find anything. So I found an employee pricing cereal boxes.

"Oh, honey, what happened to your head?" she asked.

"What?" I said. "Is there something on my head?"

We laughed, then I asked her to show me where she kept the products I needed. I bought so many bottles of Coke Zero Cherry.

This is fun, I thought. Having a wound is fun.

So I kept goofing around about my wound. I told one lady my wife hit me with a wiffle ball bat. "Who knew a wiffle ball bat could do so much damage," I said.

I told one guy it was a bug bite. That guy didn't laugh. I think he was in a bad mood.

Another guy told me how he once had a wound glued up. I told him I liked the glue, but I thought it was strange that the doctor used Elmer's glue instead of something, you know, more medical. That guy didn't laugh. He just gave me a weird look. A look that showed concern. Concern both for me and the future of healthcare.

I continued stumbling around the parking lot acting like a deranged creature. A dog barked at me. I looked over and growled at it, hoping my face would scare it. Then I noticed how cute the thing was.

"Holy fucking shit! That dog is fucking cute!" I said.

There was a woman putting groceries in the back of the jeep. She told me they just got the dog from the humane society. She told me she named it Pepper because she had always wanted to name a dog Pepper.

Then she commented on my head. "That looks like it hurts," she said.

"It's just a bug bite," I told her.

I asked if I could pet her dog.

"No," she said.

Then she got in the jeep and drove away.

AN OLD LADY sat in a shallow spot in the middle of the West River. She had a gray buzz cut and dark sunglasses and a tall can of beer. The river water broke around her like she was a rock. I said hi to her as I was prowling around.

"The water is deeper over there," she said.

I smiled and swam to the deeper section. I found the deep spot and lay on my back and let the current take me for a bit. Occasionally I probed my broken tooth with my tongue. I didn't want to go to the dentist. I just wanted to float around near drunk old ladies. Dentists look in mouths and find doom in there. This river was better. This river smelled like a river and right then I felt decent in it.

WENT TO THE dentist. I was told I
have a rotting wisdom tooth that
needs to be taken out. It had been
back there rotting away for years. I
called it the black crystal. I told my
wife I always expected it to wither
away. Just turn to dust. "Sometimes I
hate getting in your head," she told
me.

Then I had my teeth cleaned. I hadn't
been to a dentist in twenty-two years.
I was afraid once she started scraping,
bats and hornets would fly out of my
mouth. It wasn't that bad though.
There were some hard chunks of crap
that came out and now I feel like I
have a new set of teeth.

I drove back to the cabin. A storm
rolled in. There was thunder and rain.
I felt clean. I felt sweet and charming
even though all I did was nap on the
couch and listen to thunder.

I BELIEVED IN things all over again like a movie sequel that felt wrong, like it had nothing to do with the original or something like that. I believed in sandals. I believed in arguing. I believed in used books but not books that were so used they fell apart and turned into moths (well, sometimes I believed in those kinds of books that weren't even books anymore). I believed in loafing hard. I believed fashion was really, really, really ungood. I believed money gave your soul tooth decay. I believed in noisy rivers. I believed in wives and especially mine at the moment even when she thought I was being worthless. I believed in being shiftless. I believed being shiftless was a form of prayer, but even if it wasn't, I would still believe in being shiftless just cause. I liked to sit down, and watch people jump into water and laugh. I

believed in grief. I didn't believe in the
present. There were days I missed my
mom so badly it was like she had died
the day before or the day before that
or a hundred years ago or like she
never existed. But I wanted to cry for
her like she had just died and was still
rotting and looking yellow kinda. And
I thanked the good Lord for that
feeling. I believed in driving around. I
believed in butts. I believed in stinky
people. I believed in sweatshirts that
were old but have never been washed
because I believe you should never
wash a sweatshirt you really really
love.

THREE RITE AID employees stood in a line examining the candy rack. One of them was really old. The other two were teenagers. They all wore blue polo shirts and khaki slacks.

"What are you doing?" I asked. "Is there something wrong with the candy? Will the candy be alright?"

They all nodded.

"So what's happening?" I asked.

"Oh," the old one said. "We are just trying to decide what kind of candy we want."

"I would get Reese's peanut butter cups. I'm just that kind of guy."

We laughed.

"No," one of the teenagers said. "I don't want Reese's."

"Me neither," the old woman said.

But I wanted a Reese's. I wanted a peanut butter cup so badly. But I managed to restrain myself. Eating a Reese's would be the right choice spiritually, but the wrong choice for my diet.

Eventually, one of the girls grabbed a Twix then stepped behind the register and checked me out.

I drove home. I drove the speed limit. Which made the ride feel really long.

I FELL DOWN. Don't know how. I think it had something to do with my sandals. My knees hurt. No bleeding gash though. Still, I felt very clumsy.

Then I had an allergy attack. Then I drank a diet soda.

Early that day, I went swimming in the West River. I tried to float down some rapids, but they were too shallow, and I bumped my butt on many rocks.

I was a banged up guy who believed there was no other life in the galaxy. There was just us. There was nothing else out there. And that made it even more intense that I kept falling down like that.

I WENT TO the Townsend Dam and swam until my arms hurt. Then I had a candy bar for lunch. Then I went swimming again. Then I had a stomachache.

So I sat on the sand with my wife and dog. I puked a little.

"Gross, don't do that here," my wife said.

"Sorry," I said.

There was an inflatable kayak filled with teenagers. One of them had a baby. The kayak wasn't moving much because they didn't have paddles. They were all laughing and having a great time. Except the baby. The baby was crying.

I TOOK AN Ativan then I ordered new
shoes from the internet, but they
didn't fit and I napped on my old
couch which wasn't very comfortable
and I missed the solar eclipse and my
dog raced another dog in the woods
today and, because it had rained so
much that summer, the rivers and
creeks were high and loud. I don't
really need new shoes. My current
shoes looked so old. They looked like I
had been wearing them my whole life.

MY PSYCHIATRIST SMELLED really nice and she had longer legs than me and most other people too.

She was a good woman. Because of her I was able to take medicine and nap.

And I napped so many times.

And I loved goldenrod even though I was allergic to it.

And I loved swimming in cold rivers. Even though sometimes I slipped and got hurt and bled into the rushing water.

And I had a job. I took care of old people. Sometimes they watched the Weather Channel all day long. Or went outside and watched birds. This was easy and wonderful but I still got anxious then ate Ativan.

AN OLD LADY in the Rite Aid in Bellows Falls saw my butt crack sticking out. She told me I needed suspenders. "My father was also flat bottomed," she told me. "He loved wearing suspenders. It's nothing to be ashamed of." I thanked the woman for her kind advice. But I can't seem to bring myself to buy suspenders. I think they will hold my pants too high up and get them wedged up my butt crack, and that will be no good for anybody.

OUR DRIVEWAY HAD gotten bumpy. I felt like I was off-roading every time I drove up to our cabin. Sometimes I had to go to the bathroom, or I had a headache and each bump nearly destroyed me. It was an emotional thing. Once the bumps made us bounce so violently one of my wife's boobs popped out of her dress. The whole boob. We could have used this as foreplay, but I had a headache, so instead of making sweet love, I stumbled to the cabin, ate medicine, and flopped down on the couch. I called out to my wife. "PLEASE I NEED A MOIST RAG FOR MY HEAD!" She brought me a rag and placed it on my forehead gently. "THIS ISN'T MOIST. I NEED SOMETHING SO MUCH MOISTER!" I yelled. She told me I was being a baby. Then she got me a rag that was absolutely soaked. I put it on my head and felt water drip down my face. Soon the couch cushion was drenched.

WE TRIED TO put together our new bed frame. But we failed. Then I dreamed about my wife leaving me. The next day we finally got the bed made. I like our bed frame. I like how our mattress is not on the floor. It's above the floor. It feels futuristic.

WE HAD A cold week. There were patches of orange and yellow in the trees. It was sweatshirt weather. Still, I went swimming. Some friends were visiting. They swam too. One of them even got naked in the cold water. Her butt was round and made me feel good about life. It made me feel hopeful and filled with glee.

We went for a hike even though it was starting to rain. This made me grumpy. My friends teased me, and I felt loved, but still very, very grumpy.

For dinner we went to Ramuntos and ate at the bar.

There was an older couple there and they were drunk. They asked the bartender if they could order two margaritas to go.

"What do you think this is, Cancun?"
the young bartender said.

"Oh come on," the drunk old guy said.
"We aren't going to drive. We aren't
even going to walk."

No driving OR walking.

That seemed profound to me. I wanted
to do whatever it was they were doing.
It sounded spiritual. Or at least,
relaxing. I sometimes confused the
two.

That night, we drank around a fire.
After a couple beers I got heartburn.
Then I started eating Tums like it was
candy.

The next morning my friends left, and
I missed them immediately.

I went to work and watched the
Weather Channel with an old guy. I
took care of old guys for a living. That
day taking care of him meant I
watched the Weather Channel for six
hours straight.

When I got home my wife told me my
aunt Jacky had died. I didn't know
what to say. I didn't get along with my

aunt. But when I was young I thought she was wonderful. She took me to the dog track and asked me to not tell my parents. That was the first time I ever felt sneaky. And it was a great feeling. I told my parents about it as soon as I got home.

MY AUNT JACKY died. I'm going to tell you some stuff about her.

She used to party.

Once, she showed me a stack of pictures of her at a strip club with her friends. They all had beehive haircuts and were laughing wildly as men shook their penises around and flexed their muscles. At this point I was in college and drinking a lot. This was her way of bonding with me. And it worked.

She loved penguins. She had little penguin figurines all over her federal housing unit.

Even when she was broke, she made sure to send me some money on Christmas. Her cards would be taped up and hard to open. Once she gave me twenty bucks and my wife ten.

She loved talking about the past and telling stories. She was a good storyteller.

During my grandma's funeral, Jacky pointed at a man with a large nose. "That's the son of bitch who molested me when I was little," she said. "That dirty fucking perverted bastard." I kept close to her during the funeral. I kept my arm around her and leaned on her. She smelled like baby powder.

Like most of us Grimbols, she struggled with her weight her whole life.

She never married but dated many crappy men. One died on the electric chair.

When I was ten, I loved Dick Tracy and all the cool mobsters like Prune Face and Flat Top. I was obsessed. So she took me to the dog track and she would make bets for me. It felt like a real mobster-ish thing to do. I once won forty bucks, which felt like a big deal. Instead of buying a toy with the money, I had her take me to the track the next day. I lost the forty bucks and some of her money too.

She complained about my dad's second wife, Patty, constantly. The two women were enemies. They were both desperate for my father's affection. But they talked on the phone up to eight times a day. Talking that often, it didn't matter how much they resented each other. They became close. They became best friends whether they liked it or not.

I hated talking to Jacky on the phone. She'd keep me talking for hours. They were really bitter conversations that left me feeling emotionally hungover. She complained about my dead mother, saying she spoiled me and treated my father poorly. I never really got over that.

As I got older, the phone calls became more frequent and sour. I couldn't take it anymore and I stopped talking to her for a couple of years.

When I was little I'd spend hours dancing around her apartment to Michael Jackson. She'd laugh, and I would get upset and insist that she take my dancing more seriously.

She would often have a bin of Lucky Charms marshmallows for me. She would pick out all the marshmallows, not wanting me to have to bother with the cereal part.

She took me to see the movie *The Fox and The Hound* five days in a row. Then she told me we couldn't see it any more. We had seen it too many times in a row. That night I had a nightmare about *The Fox and The Hound*. In it, the Fox and the Hound never met. They never became pals. I woke up sobbing. So she drove me to the theater and we saw the twelve-thirty showing of *The Fox and The Hound*. It was a nice summer day. We were the only people in the theater.

We'd eat at McDonald's for almost every meal. Sometimes she would suggest going somewhere else. "No, I think I want McDonald's," I'd say. Every once in a while, we'd take a break from fast food and have picnics at this hill near her apartment complex.

One year, I noticed the hill looked smaller. Aunt Jacky told me it was just because I had gotten bigger. But each year, the hill became smaller and smaller. Finally, it became a small indentation in the ground. Now there is a hole there—a really deep hole. It's guarded by a flimsy wire fence.

I WOKE MY wife up and tried to convince her I was a ghost. "I've been dead for years," I told her. "You just can't deal with how I died. So you imagine I'm still here. And I am still here. But as a ghost. Why do you think I haven't made many friends in the last couple of years? It's because I'm not real. I mean, I'm a ghost. So I'm sorta real. But not fully."

She laughed. Then she noticed how naked I was.

I was extremely naked.

"Why are you naked? We had sex so long ago. Have you just been naked ever since?"

"Yes," I said. "That's what ghosts do."

"Ghosts need to shower more."

"You can't tell ghosts what to do."

"Are you stoned?"

"I can't remember. Ghosts have trouble remembering things."

MY SUIT WAS too large. The slacks were especially baggy. And I didn't have any dress shoes, so I wore sneakers. Really old and overly worn. They looked so beat up. They looked like I had been wearing them my whole life. The bride told me I looked like shit. Then she laughed. She liked to laugh at people. She had one of the best laughs I have ever experienced, so I didn't mind her laughing at me. I let her get her jokes in as a wedding present. Her actual wedding present was a check that would probably bounce, so it was good to let her have a little fun at my expense.

The wedding was held at a swanky event hall in New Jersey. There was lots of free booze. I ended up drinking too many white Russians.

At one point I ran into my buddy Ian.

He was the bride's best man. He was working on the toast and I was feeling very helpful due to all the white Russians and weed gummies.

"Dude, in your toast, you should totally talk about actual toast."

He laughed.

"Like the stuff you put butter and jelly on."

"Yeah, I get it."

I drank more white Russians then waited for the toast. Alex did not mention actual toast once. This broke my heart. I thought it was such a good idea. Now it was wasted. I was wasted. I was stumbling, and I had only had . . . I don't know how many drinks.

After the toast and dinner, the bride and groom had their first dance. Then we joined them on the dance floor. The DJs were really young and played bad music. But they had a smoke machine and I liked that. I kept asking them to shoot the smoke at my butt.

"Sure, dude," one said. "No problemo!"

They shot the smoke and I shook my butt over it. I couldn't hear much laughter. My smoky butt wasn't being appreciated. I could hear my wife laughing though. She also had a great laugh. It was loud and soulful and happy and sometimes involved hopping and clapping her hands.

I walked up to her and kissed her.

"I forgot you were here," I said.

"Oh, shut up," she said.

We danced. She had bad rhythm. Or maybe I did. I couldn't tell.

Once I got a little too sweaty, I stopped dancing and wandered around and I tried to meet some new people. Everyone wanted to know what I did for work. First, I told people my actual job title. Then I just told them I worked with old people. Then I told them I hang out with old people. Then I told them I watched the Weather Channel with old people all day long. Then I just said I watched weather. Then I just said weather. "I do the weather," I'd say. Then I told people I have anxiety issues and I take Zoloft and Ativan and nap a lot. And that was probably the most truthful thing I said that night.

Eventually, I stopped drinking and spent the rest of the night wandering around and sobering up. Around ten I drove with my wife to our hotel. I sniffed her and kissed her, and I got her into bed. During doggy style sex, I asked her to call me Donald Trump.

"What?"

"Just call me Trump, baby."

"No."

"Please?"

"No. This is weird. Why do you want me to call you that?"

"I thought it would be fun and taboo."

"Well, it's not fun."

The next day we found everyone looking hungover and slightly confused. We sat in front of the hotel. Alex had lost his wallet and his car keys and his cigarettes and one of his shoes. He looked like he was on a scavenger hunt.

My wife came over and sat on my lap.
We kissed and held each other. Then
the chair broke apart and I landed on
the ground. I couldn't stop laughing
and coughing and moaning.

"You okay?" someone asked.

"Sure," I said. "I'm just going to sit
here on the ground for a while. Shit.
Maybe I should start dieting."

"Haven't we been dieting?" Bella
asked.

"I can't remember."

For a while I worried about the hotel
charging me for the broken chair.
Then I noticed most of the hotel's
chairs were metal. I had sat in the
only wooden one.

"Hey, was that a prank chair?"

"No. That was a wedding present,"
someone said. "Don't worry though. I
got them more than one."

"Oh thank God for that."

OH MAN. I drove to the gas station in Putney because I needed gas and it was late and this was the only place that was open. The attendant was stoned and only had one eye. I gave him a twenty for gas and some more money for an Arizona Iced Tea.

"I love iced tea," he said.

"Me too," I said.

After driving for a few miles, I noticed the gas was low. At first I was confused. I had gone to the gas station. I was supposed to have gas now. Then I realized that I had forgotten to actually pump the gas. I had given the guy money and just taken my drink and driven away. My wife and I were way too broke to waste twenty bucks like that. So I sped back, and I ran to the counter and I told the attendant my problem.

"Fuck," he said. "I don't know what to do. I'm not trained for this kind of shit."

"Shit, what am I going to do? I'm so broke!"

"I don't know. I just don't know anymore."

We both started crying. And as we wept I noticed that he actually had two eyes.

Is this the right gas station? I thought.

We kept weeping.

"Hold on," the dude said. "Nobody else has been here tonight. I bet your money is still on the pump."

He looked at the screen that had top secret gas station information on it.

"Yup, your money is still on the pump. You're all set."

"Really? That's awesome."

I went out to the jeep and pumped gas.

It was dark, and the gas station looked so well lit and inviting. I looked back. The stoned attendant was standing outside smoking a cigarette. He winked at me. He winked so hard. I winked back.

FOURTEEN WILD TURKEYS marched through my front yard and somehow my dog didn't notice them. Even though I liked the turkeys, I decided to get grumpy about it. Grumpiness comes naturally to me.

"Okay, Vermont!" I yelled at the turkeys. "I get it! It's autumn! Summer's over! You've made your point! Stop rubbing it in! You don't have to be so goddamned festive all the time!"

The turkeys saw me and ran back into the woods.

This is a funky omen, I thought. Doom will happen.

Then I thought about other stuff.

Then I thought about the turkeys

again and summer ending.

Is summer over though? I don't know
if turkeys have anything to do with
summer ending. It's supposed to be a
hot week. I'll probably go swimming in
the West River. I'll smoke cigarettes
and nap. I'll probably cook a frozen
pizza. Maybe jazz it up by putting
extra cheese and sliced up garlic on it.

SUMMER WAS OVER and I desperately wanted the leaves the color of ancient married butts. Arthritic butts. I wanted leaves the color of divorce. But there was a chance we wouldn't get divorced. Maybe we would end up sleeping in different rooms. Or separate single beds. Or still be doing it every once in a while, even though we would be old. We would laugh at old sitcoms and we would gossip about long dead friends.

WE WERE IN the middle of a
heatwave. Though it was almost
October, we had a brutal week. At
night, I flailed around naked for
hours, and when I finally fell asleep, I
dreamt about sex or the end of the
world. Sometimes, when I was lucky,
I'd dream of both.

Waking up was difficult. I'd drag
myself out of bed feeling so tired I
wanted to cry. I'd eat and then head to
work, taking care of old people and
napping and cleaning their dishes and
stuff. I'd watch the Weather Channel
with this one old dude for hours. We
would hear about how the hurricanes
had damaged Florida and Puerto Rico.

I would eagerly wait for the old guy to
fall asleep. When he finally nodded off,
I would breathe a sigh of relief and
close my eyes as well. I'd nap for a bit,

and then get up and vacuum and do some dishes, make some lunch, stuff like that. I would spend an hour or so checking Facebook on my phone compulsively, even though I knew the old guy lived in the middle of nowhere and had no internet or cell reception. He still used a rotary phone, and even that technology seemed to annoy the old man. He would have gotten rid of it if he could. He'd have gotten rid of the roads too. And Bennington and Burlington and Putney. He thought those places were ruined. Too many rich people. He only liked his home and his dog and the Weather Channel, which told him about all the earthquakes and floods and tornadoes and stuff like that. He would never get rid of his TV. He needed the Weather Channel.

I THOUGHT I had a therapy appointment at three but the doors were locked. So I went to Rite Aid and got a Reese's Fast Break bar instead. I ate it and enjoyed every bite a little too much, then I decided I needed to diet. Then I went to an antique store and bought a big plastic skull covered in green glitter. Then I headed home and realized we were running low on toilet paper. I texted my wife: I forgot to buy toilet paper. It's up to you now. May God have mercy on your soul.

I TOOK HER down Putney Brook Road. It was a dirt road that twisted through a deeply wooded area. Lots of pine trees and creeks and stuff. During the first mile of our walk, I was disappointed. It wasn't dark enough. The moon was too bright. It wasn't spooky enough. My dog heard something. I told her to gear down, that it was just an owl. Then I heard some howling. And some yelping mixed in. They were coyotes and there were a lot of them. The coyote sounds got louder. My dog was scared and had her tail tucked between her legs. I stood still. They came closer. Their yelping, howling sound became strange and surly. I knew I could probably beat them up. I had a big flashlight I could use as a club. But I didn't want them to mess with my dog. And besides, I had done all my coyote research on Google. I didn't really know what it was like to fight one of these things. No. This all felt wrong. So I started running and I ran faster and for longer than I had run in a long time. Once we reached my jeep, I stopped to catch my breath. Sweat dripped down my giant forehead. I looked down at my dog. She was wagging her tail. She was wagging her whole butt. She was happy, because she loved running so much.

I STUMBLED INTO Urgent Care. The woman working the front desk had beautiful frog eyes.

"A bee stung my tongue!" I yelled.

But I was mumbling, and she couldn't understand me at first. I had to speak slowly.

"I GOT STUNG BY A BEE! ON MY TONGUE!"

"Oh. Shit. How did that happen?"

"The little fucker got in my drink. It Trojan-horsed me. I drank it then it stung me. I wasn't, like, wagging my tongue at it or anything. Sneaky bastard was in my orange juice. I drank the thing and it stung me. It hurts so bad. It even hurts my teeth and my cheeks and my throat. Ice helps though."

I put a big bag of ice on the counter.

"Where did you get that?"

"Rite Aid."

She laughed.

"That's a big bag of ice."

"I know."

I filled out some paperwork then waited an hour or so. I kept eating ice. My tongue was cold.

Eventually I saw this frumpy doctor guy. He was friendly. Told me my throat was swelling. The pain was just nerves. We joked around and laughed. I felt like I was in therapy.

"It just hurts so bad," I kept saying.

"I'm sure," he said.

"Will the pain ever go away?"

"Sure. In a few hours. Just keep eating ice. I'll write you a prescription for another bag."

We laughed. I almost hugged him. He hadn't done much. But I felt like we were best friends.

I kept eating ice then went home. I had forgotten I had a meeting with my therapist. There was a message from her on my answering machine. She sounded worried.

"I DON'T LIKE Vermont food. They have too many bees in their orange juice."

"Can't argue with that."

I spent most of the day telling people about the bee that stung my tongue.

"It hurt all day. I had to eat so much ice," I told one guy.

"I love ice," he said.

Also the colors of the leaves had gotten darker. Some were the color of a rusty wagon. Others were the color of someone who was very old and very tan. Some were the color of a street light that was ancient and flickering.

Some trees had lost all their leaves.

Also, apple cider tasted so good. Sometimes, when I drank it, I moaned.

BEFORE THE POETRY reading, I took a shower and put so much shampoo in my hair. I thought it would help me sell books. Once, when I was twelve, I ate a tube of toothpaste before a party cause I wanted to make out with everyone ever. It didn't work. Nobody kissed me even a little bit. Anyway, I didn't know if the shampoo helped sales. I sold a couple of books, I think. And the reading went well. People laughed at my jokes. I mean my poetry. I mean my paragraphs. I mean, my writing stuff. I mean, afterwards I got drunk on white Russians and, on our way home, I used a baby voice and told my wife I loved her and that she was soooo pretty and that she was also terrifying and mad at me too much, but I loved her soooo much anyway. She got annoyed and told me to shut up. I didn't. I kept talking about love and terror.

A BUNCH OF old ladies sat on the top of Putney Mountain. They had binoculars to look at the mountains, which were covered in red, orange, and brown leaves.

I was there too, just sweating. I hadn't hiked in a while and I felt really out of shape. My dog was with me. She ate something off the ground. I reached into her mouth and pulled it out. At first it looked like a rock. Then I noticed it was rubbery. I peeled it apart. It looked like pork or chicken maybe.

"Mystery meat!" the old ladies yelled.

They all laughed.

I laughed with the old ladies for a bit.

Then I headed back down to my car

and drove to my friend's bookstore. We joked about the reading I gave and how drunk I had gotten. "You were really sweet," the guy told me. "Some people get mean when they are drunk. But you just got sweet. You were a fucking candy cane man."

I hung out there and talked about books for a while. My dog was outside tied to a railing. She was enjoying the sun.

I WENT SHOPPING at Aldi. The food was so cheap there, and the cashiers worked so fast. I loved watching them. I told this one cashier how impressed I was.

"You should have a competition and see who moves the fastest," I told her.

"Oh trust me," she said. "We know. Management keeps track of everything and they make us very aware of our performance level."

"Shit," I said. "So who is the fastest?"

"You don't wanna know," she said.

Then we laughed.

I thought it was a funny thing to say. I didn't know anyone who worked there. Why would it matter if she told me?

I do know this. I have bought many frozen pizzas from that place. And I like to put garlic and diced up peppers and pesto and extra cheese on them.

I PASSED BY a dog on Patch Rd. She was big and fat and bumbling around the yellow lines looking lost. So I pulled over and got out. The fat old lady dog ran up to me and jumped up and tried to lick me. Then she ran around my car a few times. I tried to catch her and look at her collar. Hopefully find an address. She ran up to me again. I leaned over. She licked my face and then ran around my car some more. I tried to run after her. She ran into the woods, her tail wagging. When I got back into my car, I felt a surge of emotion. I started crying. I couldn't believe the old lost dog had gotten to me so badly. I couldn't believe I had become the type of guy who cries so easily. But I was also grateful for that.

MY FIRST WIFE and only wife (so far) asked me to pick up toilet paper. Then, while I was out for a drive, she texted me: DONT FORGET TO PICK UP TOILET PAPER.

Then I texted back: I AM TOTALLY GOING TO FORGET TO PICK UP TOILET PAPER.

Then, once I got home, I realized I actually forgot to pick up the toilet paper!

I could have gone and picked some up but I was afraid I'd be out there, roaming around, looking at leaves that looked like a chain-smoking sunset, and I would feel lost, or something.

I GREW UP in Sag Harbor, New York eating Conca D'Oro pizza. As a young puberty face, I wandered around town bumming money from rich people just to get a slice. My cousin called and told me the place had closed, and I became sad. I missed the last day because I moved around too often and was a chronic broke ass and had too much grief. But my cousin lived there and he told me all about it. There was a new owner and he was changing the name to Sag Pizza. That was the worst name I had ever heard. Oh lord. Conca . . . closed. My soul felt ingrown and lousy and too far away. I remembered the last time I ate there. I hadn't been to Sag Harbor in years. The owner, Frank, gave me this look that said: Hey, it's you, I haven't seen you in a while. And a while could have been a week, or a few months, or a few years, or an eternity.

I WAS MAKING this old guy breakfast when, out of the kitchen window, I saw a bear run across his yard. It stopped for a moment and looked back at the house. I told the old guy there was a bear and he stood up and looked out the window with me.

"Too bad you're not a camera," he said.

"What?"

"I was wondering if you had a camera."

The bear was gone now. It was fat but quick.

ONE OF MY clients asked me to chase
a duck off his pond.

"This isn't a goddamned duck pond,"
the old man said.

I have a list of things I'm supposed to
help the dude with. Cleaning, hygiene,
cooking, cleaning. I'm not supposed to
be chasing ducks. But he was nice and
usually we spent our days listening to
classical music in his dusty little
cabin. We napped. I read and got some
writing done.

He was a good man.

So I decided to do the old guy a favor
and chase the duck away. Oh man. I
was way too slow. I'd run to one side of
the pond. He would swim to the other.
I threw dirt. The duck dodged it.

At one point I accidentally fell into the pond. I got soaked.

Eventually I gave up, got some new clothes out of my jeep and stumbled back into the cabin.

"I failed," I told my client. "The duck is too tricky. I need a tranquilizer gun. A jeep. A net. A safari helmet."

"Ducks are tricky. Maybe that bear will come back and eat him."

"We can only hope," I said.

Then I sat back and listened to Aaron Copland's "Fanfare for the Common Man."

IT HAD BEEN snowing. Not much.
Just flurries. No accumulation.

I hated the holidays. They made me
really moody.

I knew I needed to visit my dad
though. He was like a hundred years
old or something. Or maybe in his
seventies.

His gallbladder was recently removed
because it was covered in gangrene. I
had to visit. He lived in Wisconsin. It
was flat there. It had corn.

THANKSGIVING AT MY mother-in-law's left me curvy and old and a little too stoned and I was fat and bearded and thankful for things like beach-walking and tall grass filled with birds giving birth and frothing ocean and weed to smoke and Zoloft and all kinds of weird sex that smelled like taxi cabs, and my dad, who was lonely, and my mom, who was lonely in more of a dead sort of way. And I was thankful for showers and penises brushing up against other penises and gas stations and driftwood and sitcoms and gossip and blankets and board games and antique stores and bad dreams and sweatpants and my wife's curvy everything and for books, even the bad ones, and banana cream pie, even though it made me feel full and sick. And I was thankful to watch *Seinfeld* with my brother-in-law and smoke more weed. And I was thankful for Jesus stuff, like the meek will inherit stuff and whatnot. Most of the time, the soul preferred bad advice and greasy conversations and I spent most of the summer and fall dreading winter, and now I looked forward to seeing tire tracks in the snow and grabbing my steering wheel tightly while driving five miles per hour through a storm.

ON MY WAY to work, I saw this woman stumbling down the road wearing nothing but a nightgown. It was cold. Maybe thirty degrees out. This poor old woman was barefoot. There wasn't anything around for miles, so I turned around and asked her if she needed help. She came up to my jeep.

"What did you say?" she asked.

She wasn't old. Just skinny and strung out.

"I was just wondering if you are okay."

"I'm fine. It's beautiful out."

I smiled, then turned back around and headed for work. The old guy I was taking care of played the TV and the radio at the same time. The radio played classical music. The TV showed models pretending to be funny or normal or in the future or whatever. Then the football game came on.

WEED HAPPENED. Then I bought an expensive poetry book at the bookstore. Then I just hung out there for a long time. Then the owners of the bookstore and my wife and I got Chinese Food Buffet. I ate too much. Winter was coming. Things were going to get slippery.

WEEKS PASSED. The leaves had fallen. So it was winter. Kinda. I could hear gunshots in the woods. My wife was still curvy. Might get curvier. I was curvy too, but in a less good way.

WE DROVE TO Upstate New York for our friend's wedding. She looked beautiful and she couldn't stop crying. She stood up there with her fiancé and tears dripped from her face. She was like the best kind of leaky faucet. I read a poem I had written for her. It was about those tears. I knew those tears. I have known her and those tears since they were young.

After the service we went to a restaurant and I drank too many white Russians. My wife got really mad at me.

"You were supposed to drive tonight," she said. "You promised you would stay sober and drive."

"I forgot," I said. "But come on. It's not such a big deal. Wasn't my poem good?"

"You have three hours to get your ass sober," she said.

So I went outside and tried to puke into the snow. A biker came out and asked me if I was alright. I explained my situation.

"Oh shit, man," he said. "You got to really puke it up. Stick like three fingers in there."

I took his advice.

"Come on!" he yelled. "You can do it! Harder! Faster!"

Tired from puking, I stumbled back into the restaurant and found a quiet corner and napped on the floor for a couple of hours.

When I woke up, I was sober.

The next day we drove home. It had snowed while we were gone. I tried to drive up the driveway. But I couldn't do it. The jeep slid backwards. I almost got us stuck but I was able to straighten the jeep out and then back down.

The next day I bought some groceries.
I didn't want to carry the groceries up
the hill, so I put the pedal to the metal
and managed to launch the jeep up
the driveway. I felt so proud of myself.
I forgot how satisfying it was to drive
up that icy driveway. I felt so good
about life and love and marriage even.

HERE IS THE poem I read at the wedding:

SOME BAD ADVICE ABOUT
MARRIAGE

Argue as much as possible
Argue about arguing.

Don't be afraid to cook up a frozen
pizza every once in a while

Let the dishes stack up

Fear teenagers

Fortify your home with gardens
Grow basil please
Grow skin tags too

When you are in the car, take off your
wedding ring

And pretend to throw it
Out the window. Then smile.
And turn the music up. Sing together.

Sing a song you don't really know the
lyrics to.

Watch sappy movies. Laugh at
whoever cries first.

Once your kid is a teenager,
Stay up late gossiping with each other
Even if you have work in the morning.

Make important decisions by playing
Rock Paper Scissors Shoot

Remember, getting old isn't so bad
We would all be lucky to end up
Like those run-down cars you find
In the middle of the woods.

I knew this girl in college
She was beautiful and
Cried a lot
She cried when she was sad
And when she was laughing
She even cried
When she
Was content
Or making soup.
She had watery eyes

And I would hang out with her
And think oh man this girl
Is going to be a great mom
Because she cried a lot and my
Mom also cried a lot even though
It was over different things,
So now I can't help but to relate
Tears to moms and strength
And all that

Because
The west coast is on fire
And the internet is angry
And there are stray dogs
And churches turned into
Thrift stores.

But

There are also homes out there
Surrounded by rich soil
Leased to farmers
Who grow tall stalks of corn.
Once the corn is harvested
You can see the house at night
The lights are on late. The whole
family
Has decided to skip their own bedtime
They will wake up tired
But still have to go to work in the
morning.

Justin Grimbol lives in Vermont with his wife and dog.

Other **Atlatl Press** Books

Giraffe Carcass by J. Peter W.

Shining the Light by A.S. Coomer

Failure As a Way of Life by Andersen Prunty

Hold for Release Until the End of the World
by C.V. Hunt

Die Empty by Kirk Jones

Mud Season by Justin Grimbol

Death Metal Epic (Book Two: Goat Song Sacrifice)
by Dean Swinford

Come Home, We Love You Still by Justin Grimbol

We Did Everything Wrong by C.V. Hunt

Squirm With Me by Andersen Prunty

Hard Bodies by Justin Grimbol

Arafat Mountain by Mike Kleine

Drinking Until Morning by Justin Grimbol

Thanks For Ruining My Life by C.V. Hunt

Death Metal Epic (Book One: The Inverted Katabasis)
by Dean Swinford

Fill the Grand Canyon and Live Forever by Andersen Prunty

Mastodon Farm by Mike Kleine

Fuckness by Andersen Prunty

Losing the Light by Brian Cartwright

They Had Goat Heads by D. Harlan Wilson

The Beard by Andersen Prunty

27362396R00094

Made in the USA
Middletown, DE
19 December 2018